Dear Parent:
Your child's love of reading starts here!

Every child learns to read in a different way and at his or her own speed. You can help your young reader improve and become more confident by encouraging his or her own interests and abilities. You can also guide your child's spiritual development by reading stories with biblical values and Bible stories, like I Can Read! books published by Zonderkidz. From books your child reads with you to the first books he or she reads alone, there are I Can Read! books for every stage of reading:

SHARED READING
Basic language, word repetition, and whimsical illustrations, ideal for sharing with your emergent reader.

BEGINNING READING
Short sentences, familiar words, and simple concepts for children eager to read on their own.

READING WITH HELP
Engaging stories, longer sentences, and language play for developing readers.

READING ALONE
Complex plots, challenging vocabulary, and high-interest topics for the independent reader.

ADVANCED READING
Short paragraphs, chapters, and exciting themes for the perfect bridge to chapter books.

I Can Read! books have introduced children to the joy of reading since 1957. Featuring award-winning authors and illustrators and a fabulous cast of beloved characters, I Can Read! books set the standard for beginning readers.

A lifetime of discovery begins with the magical words "I Can Read!"

Visit www.icanread.com for information on enriching your child's reading experience.
Visit www.zonderkidz.com for more Zonderkidz I Can Read! titles.

There is a time for everything,
and a season for every
activity under the heavens.

—*Ecclesiastes 3:1*

ZONDERKIDZ

The Berenstain Bears® God Made the Seasons
Copyright © 2012 by Berenstain Publishing, Inc.
Illustrations © 2012 by Berenstain Publishing, Inc.

Requests for information should be addressed to:
Zonderkidz, *Grand Rapids, Michigan 49530*

ISBN 978-0-310-72509-1

Editor: *Mary Hassinger*
Design: *Diane Mielke*

Printed in China

12 13 14 15 16 /DSC/ 10 9 8 7 6 5 4 3 2 1

I Can Read!

BEGINNING
1
READING

The Berenstain Bears®

God Made the Seasons

Story and Pictures By

Stan & Jan Berenstain with Mike Berenstain

Living Lights™

ZONDERVAN.com/
AUTHORTRACKER
follow your favorite authors

4

God made the seasons, four in all,
winter, spring, summer, and fall.
In winter we are always told
to put on hats or we'll get cold.

When we go out,

we see our breath.

We see our friends

Fred and Beth.

The snow and ice
are really great!
We can sled!
We can skate!

Mama can do
a figure eight.
Hooray for Mama!
Isn't she great?

Papa, stop!

That ice is thin.

Don't skate there.

You may fall in!

The Bible says, "The winter is past."

Thank you, God. Spring, at last!

Soon signs of spring begin to show.

Bits of green grow through the snow.

Crocuses begin to peep,
waking from their winter sleep.

We see one with a yellow face.
We see robins find a nesting
place.

Robins build a nest
of grass and twigs.

Then Daddy Robin
digs and digs.

He digs for worms
in our yard.
The ground is still
cold and hard.

He finds a worm!
He gets lucky!

You may think that
worms are yucky.

But to robins
they are yummy!
Just right for
a robin's tummy!

God's bright sun climbs high in the sky.

Mom says spring's the reason why.

We get out bikes.

We put back sleds.

Mama weeds the flower beds.

Now the sun is overhead.

Now it's summer, Mama said.

God makes the sun warm all the earth,

and the earth makes plants for all it's worth!

Flowers!

How their colors glow!

You can almost

see them grow!

Mama makes some
lemonade.

We will drink it in the shade.

Thank you, God, for all

summer brings—

for lemonade, shade, and

birds that sing!

Here's the lake

where we all swim.

Brother's slow.

I yell at him.

Come on, Brother!

Shake a leg!

Last one in

is a rotten egg!

We swim.

We float.

We wave to someone
in a boat.

We see a fish.

We see a frog.

Look! Is that
an alligator?

No. It's just
a floating log!

"Come out," says Mama.

"You've had enough!"

The clouds float by,
puff by puff.

"Let there be light," the Bible said.

A great big light is overhead.

We feel the sun on our backs.

We eat berries for our snacks.

We feel a breeze.

It's getting cool.

We'll soon be going

back to school.

Summertime is almost gone.

The seasons just keep moving on.

God made the seasons—one, two, three.

What's number four? Now, let us see.

The color of leaves
turns bright and bold.
Yellow!
Red!   Orange!
Gold!

Fall is here!

It's all around!

Leaves are falling to the ground!

Winter's coming.
And we all know
what trees stay green
in the snow!

Christmas trees
remind us, friends,
that very soon
the whole year ends.

It's the season of the
Christ Child's birth,
a season of joy for
all the earth.
But, after Christmas,
we will still be here,
all set to start
a brand-new year!

A LITTLE SPOT STAYS HOME

A STORY ABOUT VIRUSES AND SAFE DISTANCING

To all the essential workers
who are keeping us SAFE!

This book belongs to:

_____

_____

_____

Hi, I'm a little
SAFETY SPOT!

I'm here to help you stay SAFE when
a VIRUS starts spreading too fast and
gets a lot of people very sick.

Use Soap

Wash your hands really well for at least 20 seconds (sing the Happy Birthday song twice).

That's why it's so important to wash your hands to clean off GERMS before you eat, after you go to the bathroom, and after you're done playing.

When a VIRUS enters your body, you can start to have SYMPTOMS.

SYMPTOMS don't make you feel very good. They can be a fever, a cough, and a sore throat. People can spread a VIRUS more when they have SYMPTOMS, because GERMS come out of their nose and mouth when they cough or sneeze.

Sore Throat

Cough

Fever

If you become sick, you should stay at home or go to the doctor, which can help prevent others from getting ill.

If you are having
SYMPTOMS, wearing a MASK is a great way to prevent the VIRUS from spreading. This also shows you are being KIND by not wanting to spread GERMS to others.

If you are healthy, wearing a MASK can protect you if you are around someone who is coughing and sneezing.

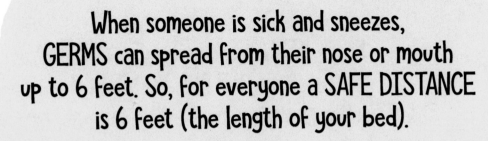

When someone is sick and sneezes,
GERMS can spread from their nose or mouth
up to 6 feet. So, for everyone a SAFE DISTANCE
is 6 feet (the length of your bed).

If you don't have a tissue, you should always
cough and sneeze into your upper sleeve
or inner elbow.

SAFE DISTANCE = 6 feet long
YOUR BED = 6 feet long

Some VIRUSES can be VERY CONTAGIOUS and cause an OUTBREAK. When this happens, older adults, like grandmas and grandpas, as well as people with low or compromised immune systems, can get sick VERY EASILY, and it can be very harmful.

We need to be RESPONSIBLE and help protect them. We can do this by handwashing and limiting contact with others by keeping a SAFE DISTANCE.

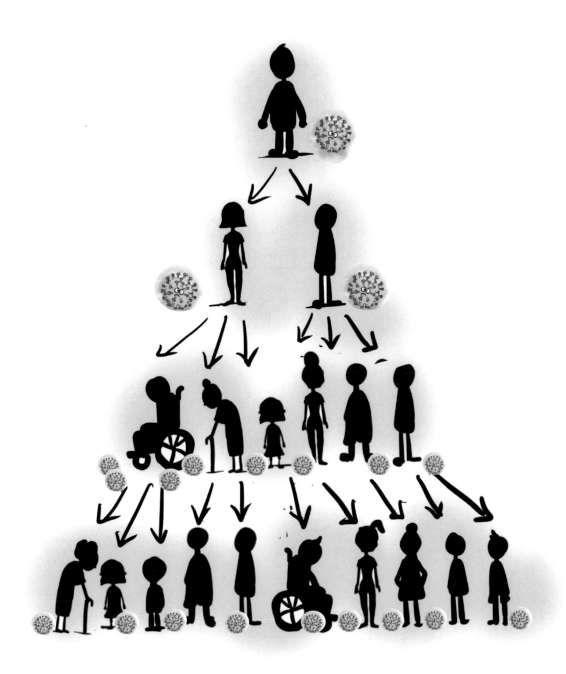

During an OUTBREAK, if SAFE DISTANCING doesn't slow down the VIRUS fast enough, everyone will need to STAY HOME. This means no parties or seeing friends or extended family. Schools may also be closed for a while, too. This is called a STAY AT HOME ORDER.

When everyone STAYS HOME, doctors have time to find out more about the VIRUS and prepare for patients. It also helps them find a treatment that can help before the VIRUS hurts a lot of people.

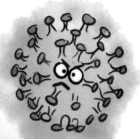

Great question!
You can go for a walk with your immediate family as long as you are at a SAFE DISTANCE from others.

People can also leave their homes if it is absolutely necessary, like to get food, go to the doctor, or if their job is considered essential.

Essential workers need to be at work to help keep us safe. They help treat sick people and deliver and stock important items.

These people are doctors, nurses, police officers, grocery store workers, and delivery workers, just to name a few. We should be very THANKFUL for these people who have the COURAGE to go to work every day!

What are essential workers?

Essential Workers

This time can be difficult for a lot of us and getting a letter in the mail can brighten someone's day!

You can learn a new skill.

Or spend extra time with your immediate family!

It can inspire you to be CREATIVE!

Or encourage you to get ORGANIZED and tackle new projects!

What do you love most about spending time at home?

_____

_____

_____

_____

_____

_____

This sheet and more great resources are available to download
for FREE! Visit: www.dianealber.com

Made in the USA
Middletown, DE
04 September 2020